THE ELUSIVE BULLET

BY

CECIL STREET
'JOHN RHODE'

British Library Cataloguing-in-Publication Data
A catalogue record for this book is available from
the British Library

Contents

CECIL STREET

Cecil John Charles Street – who wrote under a range of interlinked pseudonyms, primarily 'John Rhode' – was born in Gibraltar in 1884. He spent the early portion of his life living in Surrey, and then Berkshire, where he attended Wellington College. Street then entered the military as an artillery officer in the British army. During World War I, he became a propagandist for MI7, rising to the rank of Major. After the armistice, he switched between Dublin and London during the Irish War of Independence as Information Officer for Dublin Castle.

Street began writing somewhere around the age of thirty, starting off with non-fiction works on politics and criminology, before becoming a prolific producer of straightforward detective stories in the tradition of Freeman Wills Crofts. Street's two main fiction series are the 'Dr Lancelot Priestley' books under the name of John Rhode, and the 'Inspector Henry Arnold' books under the name of Miles Burton. Over the course of his life, Street produced some 140 novels and a number of short stories. Critically, opinion on his work tends to be divided: Some consider a number of his novels classics of scientific detection, while critics such as Julian Symons consider him part of the 'Humdrum' school of detective fiction, stating that Street "came late to writing fiction," and lacked "much talent for it."

Amongst Street's most enduring works are the short stories 'The Elusive Bullet' (1931) and 'The Purple Line' (1950 – both unusual in that they are solved through mathematical analysis, a rarity in mystery fiction – and the novels *The Claverton Affair* (1933) and *Death in Harley Street* (1946).

The Elusive Bullet

JOHN RHODE

'BY THE WAY, professor, there's something in the evening papers that might interest you,' said Inspector Hanslet, handing over as he spoke the copy he had been holding in his hand. 'There you are, "Prominent City Merchant found dead". Read it, it sounds quite interesting.'

Dr Priestley adjusted his spectacles and began to read the paragraph. The professor and myself, Harold Merefield, who had been his secretary for a couple of years, had been sitting in the study of Dr Priestley's house in Westbourne Terrace, one fine June evening after dinner, when Inspector Hanslet had been announced. The inspector was an old friend of ours, who availed himself of the professor's hobby, which was the mathematical detection of crime, to discuss with him any investigations upon which he happened to be engaged. He had just finished giving the professor an outline of a recent burglary case, over which the police had confessed themselves puzzled, and had risen to go, when the item in the newspaper occurred to him.

'This does not appear to me to be particularly interesting,' said the professor. 'It merely states that on the arrival of the 3.20 train this afternoon at Tilbury station a porter, in examining the carriages, found the dead body of a man, since identified as a Mr Farquharson, lying in a corner of a first-class carriage. This Mr Farquharson appears to have met his death through a blow on the side of the head although no weapon capable of inflicting such a blow has so far been found. I can only suggest that if the facts are as reported, there are at least a dozen theories which could be made to fit in with them.'

'Such as?' inquired Hanslet tentatively.

The professor frowned. 'You know perfectly well, inspector, that I most strongly deprecate all conjecture,' he replied severely. 'Conjecture, unsupported by a thorough examination of facts, has been responsible for more than half the errors made by mankind throughout the ages. But, to demonstrate my meaning, I will outline a couple of theories which fit in with all the reported facts. Mr Farquharson may have been struck by an assailant who left the train before its arrival at Tilbury, and who disposed of the weapon in some way. On the other hand, he may have leant out of the window, and been struck by some object at the side of the line, or even by a passing train, if he was at the right-hand side of the carriage, looking in the direction in which the train was going. Of course, as I wish to emphasize, a knowledge of *all* the facts, not only those contained in this brief paragraph, would probably render both these theories untenable.'

Hanslet smiled. He knew well enough from experience the professor's passion for facts and his horror of conjecture.

'Well, I don't suppose the case will come my way,' he said

as he turned towards the door. 'But if it does I'll let you know what transpires. I shouldn't wonder if we know the whole story in a day or two. It looks simple enough. Well good night, sir.'

The professor waited till the front door had closed behind him. 'I have always remarked that Hanslet's difficulties are comparatively easy of solution, but that what he calls simple problems completely baffle his powers of reasoning. I should not be surprised if we heard from him again very shortly.'

As usual, the professor was right. Hanslet's first visit had been on Saturday evening. On the following Tuesday, at about the same time, he called again, with a peculiarly triumphant expression on his face.

'You remember that Farquharson business, don't you, professor?' he began without preliminary. 'Well, it did come my way, after all. The Essex police called Scotland Yard in, and I was put on to it. I've solved the whole thing in under forty-eight hours. Not a bad piece of work eh? Mr Farquharson was murdered by—'

Dr Priestley held up his hand protestingly. 'My dear inspector, I am not the least concerned with the murderer of this Mr Farquharson. As I have repeatedly told you my interest in these matters is purely theoretical, and confined to the processes of deduction. You are beginning your story at the wrong end. If you wish me to listen to it, you must first tell me the full facts, then explain the course of your investigations, step by step.'

'Very well, sir,' replied Hanslet, somewhat crestfallen. 'The first fact I learnt was how Farquharson was killed. It appeared at first sight that he had been struck a terrific blow by some weapon like a pole-axe. There was a wound about two inches across on the right side of his head. But, at the post-mortem, this was found to have been caused by a bullet from an ordinary service rifle, which was found embedded in his brain.'

'Ah!' remarked the professor. 'A somewhat unusual instrument of murder, surely? What position did the body occupy in the carriage when it was found?'

'Oh, in the right-hand corner, facing the engine, I believe,' replied Hanslet impatiently. ' But that's of no importance, as you'll see. The next step, obviously, was to find out something about Farquharson, and why any one should want to murder him. The discovery of a motive is a very great help in an investigation like this. Farquharson lived with his daughter in a biggish house near a place called Stanford-le-Hope, on the line between Tilbury and Southend. On Saturday last he left his office, which is close to Fenchurch Street station, about one o'clock. He lunched at a restaurant near by, and caught the 2.15 at Fenchurch Street. As this was the train in which his dead body was found, I need hardly detail the inquiries by which I discovered these facts.'

The professor nodded. 'I am prepared to take your word for them,' he said.

'Very well, now let us come to the motive,' continued Hanslet. 'Farquharson was in business with his nephew, a rather wild young fellow named Robert Halliday. It seems that this young man's mother, Farquharson's sister, had a good deal of money in the business, and was very anxious that her son should carry it on after Farquharson's death. She died a couple of years ago, leaving rather a curious will, by which all her money was to remain in her brother's business, and was to revert to her son only at her brother's death.'

The professor rubbed his hands. 'Ah, the indispensable motive begins to appear!' he exclaimed with a sarcastic smile. 'I am sure that you feel that no further facts are necessary, inspector. It follows, of course, that young Halliday murdered his uncle to secure the money. You described him as a wild young man, I think? Really, the evidence is most damning!'

'It's all very well for you to laugh at me, professor,' replied

Hanslet indignantly. 'I'll admit that you've given me a line on things that I couldn't find for myself often enough. But in this case there's no possible shadow of doubt about what happened. What would you say if I told you that Halliday actually travelled in the very train in which his uncle's body was found?'

'Speaking without a full knowledge of the facts, I should say that this rather tended to establish his innocence,' said the professor gravely.

Hanslet winked knowingly. ' Ah, but that's by no means all,' he replied. 'Halliday is a Territorial, and he left London on Saturday afternoon in uniform, and carrying a rifle. It seems that, although he's very keen, he's a shocking bad marksman, and a member of a sort of awkward squad which goes down occasionally to Purfleet ranges to practise. Purfleet is a station between London and Tilbury. Halliday got out there, fired a number of rounds, and returned to London in the evening.'

'Dear, dear, I'm sorry for that young man,' remarked the professor. 'First we have a motive, then an opportunity. Of course, he travelled in the same carriage as his uncle, levelled his musket at his head, inflicted a fearful wound, and decamped. Why, there's hardly a weak link in the whole chain.'

'It wasn't quite as simple as that,' replied Hanslet patiently. 'He certainly didn't travel in the same carriage as his uncle, since that very morning they had quarrelled violently. Farquharson, who was rather a strict old boy, didn't approve of his nephew's ways. Not that I can find out much against him, but he's a bit of a young blood, and his uncle didn't like it. He travelled third class, and swears that he didn't know his uncle was on the train.'

'Oh, you have interviewed him already, have you?' said the professor quietly.

'I have,' replied Hanslet. 'His story is that he nearly missed the train, jumped into it at the last moment, in fact. Somewhere after Barking he found himself alone, and that's all he told me. When I asked him what he was doing scrambling along the footboard outside the train between Dagenham and Rainham, he became very confused, and explained that on putting his head out of the window he had seen another member of the awkward squad a few carriages away, and made up his mind to join him. He gave me the man's name, and when I saw him he confirmed Halliday's story.'

'Really, inspector, your methods are masterly,' said the professor. 'How did you know that he had been on the footboard?'

'A man working on the line had seen a soldier in uniform, with a rifle slung over his back, in this position,' replied Hanslet triumphantly.

'And you immediately concluded that this man must be Halliday,' commented the professor. 'Well, guesses must hit the truth sometimes, I suppose. What exactly is your theory of the crime?'

'It seems plain enough,' replied Hanslet. 'Halliday had watched his uncle enter the train, then jumped into a carriage close to his. At a predetermined spot he clambered along with his loaded rifle, shot him through the window, then, to avert suspicion, joined his friend, whom he had also seen enter the train, a little further on. It's as plain as a pikestaff to me.'

'So it appears,' remarked the professor dryly. 'What steps do you propose to take in the matter?'

'I propose to arrest Halliday at the termination of the inquest,' replied Hanslet complacently.

The professor made no reply to this for several seconds. 'I think it would be to everybody's advantage if you consulted me again before doing so,' he said at last.

A cloud passed for an instant over Hanslet's face. 'I will, if you think it would do any good,' he replied. 'But you must see for yourself that I have enough evidence to secure a conviction from any jury.'

'That is just what disquiets me,' returned the professor quickly. 'You cannot expect the average juryman to have an intelligence superior to yours, you know. I have your promise?'

'Certainly, if you wish it,' replied Hanslet rather huffily. He changed the subject abruptly, and a few minutes later he rose and left the house.

In the course of our normal routine I forgot the death of Mr Farquharson entirely. It was not until the following afternoon, when Mary the parlourmaid entered the study with the announcement that a Miss Farquharson had called and begged that she might see the professor immediately, that the matter recurred to me.

'Miss Farquharson!' I exclaimed. 'Why, that must be the daughter of the fellow who was murdered the other day. Hanslet said he had a daughter, you remember.'

'The balance of probability would appear to favour that theory,' replied the professor acidly. 'Yes, I'll see her. Show Miss Farquharson in, please, Mary.'

Miss Farquharson came in, and the professor greeted her with his usual courtesy. 'To what do I owe the pleasure of this visit?' he inquired.

Miss Farquharson hesitated a moment or two before she replied. She was tall and fair, dressed in deep mourning with an elusive prettiness which I, at least, found most attractive. And even before she spoke, I guessed something of the truth from the flush which suffused her face at the professor's question.

'I'm afraid you may think this an unpardonable intrusion,' she said at last. ' The truth is that Bob – Mr Halliday – who is my cousin, has heard of you and begged me to come and see you.'

The professor frowned. He hated his name becoming known in connection with any of the investigations which he undertook, but in spite of all his efforts, many people had come to know of his hobby. Miss Farquharson took his frown for a sign of disapproval, and continued with an irresistible tone of pleading in her voice.

'It was only as a last hope I came to you,' she said. 'It's all so awful that I feel desperate. I expect you know that my father was found dead last Saturday in a train at Tilbury, while he was on his way home?'

The professor nodded. 'I am aware of some of the facts,' he replied non-committally. 'I need not trouble you to repeat them. But in what way can I be of assistance to you?'

'It's too terrible!' she exclaimed with a sob. 'The police suspect Bob of having murdered him. They haven't said so, but they have been asking him all sorts of dreadful questions. Bob thought perhaps you might be able to do something—'

Her voice tailed away hopelessly under the professor's unwinking gaze.

'My dear young lady, I am not a magician,' he replied. 'I may as well tell you that I have seen Inspector Hanslet who has what he considers a convincing case against your cousin.'

'But you don't believe it, do you, Doctor Priestley?' interrupted Miss Farquharson eagerly.

'I can only accept the inspector's statements as he gave them to me,' replied the professor. 'I know nothing of the case beyond what he has told me. Perhaps you would allow me to ask you a few questions?'

'Of course!' she exclaimed. 'I'll tell you everything I can.'

The professor inclined his head with a gesture of thanks. 'Was your father in the habit of travelling by the 2.15 train from Fenchurch Street on Saturday afternoons?'

'No,' replied Miss Farquharson with decision. 'Only when he was kept later than usual at the office. His usual custom was to come home to a late lunch.'

'I see. Now, can you tell me the reason for the quarrel between him and your cousin?'

This time Miss Farquharson's reply was not so prompt. She lowered her head so that we could not see her face, and kept silence for a moment. Then, as though she had made up her mind, she spoke suddenly.

'I see no harm in telling you. As a matter of fact, Bob and I have been in love with one another for a long time, and Bob decided to tell my father on Saturday morning. Father was rather old-fashioned, and he didn't altogether approve of Bob. Not that there was any harm in anything he did, but father couldn't understand that a young man liked to amuse himself. There was quite a scene when Bob told him, and father refused to hear anything about it until Bob had reformed, as he put it. But I know that Bob didn't kill him,' she concluded entreatingly. 'It's impossible for anybody who knew him to believe he could. You don't believe it, do you?'

'No, I do not believe it,' replied the professor slowly. 'If it is any consolation to you and Mr Halliday, I may tell you in confidence that I never have believed it. When is the inquest to be?'

A look of deep thankfulness overspread her features. 'I am more grateful to you than I can say, Doctor Priestley,' she said earnestly. ' The inquest? On Saturday morning. Will you be there?'

The professor shook his head. 'No, I shall not be there,' he replied. 'You see, it is not my business. But I shall take steps before then to make certain inquiries. I do not wish to raise your hopes unduly, but it is possible that I may be able to divert suspicion from Mr Halliday. More than that I cannot say.'

Tears of thankfulness came to her eyes. 'I can't tell you what this means to Bob and me,' she said. 'He has been terribly distressed. He quite understands that things look very black against him, and he cannot suggest who could have wanted to kill my father. Father hadn't an enemy in the world, poor dear.'

'You are sure of that?' remarked the professor.

'Quite,' she replied positively. 'I knew every detail of his life, he never hid the smallest thing from me.'

And after a further short and unimportant conversation she took her leave of us.

The professor sat silent for some minutes after her departure. 'Poor girl!' he said at last. 'To lose her father so tragically, and then to see the man she loves accused of his murder! We must see what we can do to help her, Harold. Get me the one-inch map of the country between London and Tilbury, and a time-table of the Southend trains.'

I hastened to obey him, and for an hour or more he pored over the map, working upon it with a rule and a protractor. At the end of this period he looked up and spoke abruptly.

'This is remarkably interesting, more so than I imagined at first it would be. Run out and buy me the sheets of the six-inch survey which cover Rainham and Purfleet. I think we shall need them.'

I bought the maps he required and returned with them. For the rest of the day he busied himself with these, and it was not until late in the evening that he spoke to me again.

'Really, my boy, this problem is beginning to interest me,' he said. 'There are many points about it which are distinctly baffling. We must examine the country on the spot. There is a train to Purfleet, I see, at 10.30 tomorrow morning.'

'Have you formed any theory, sir?' I inquired eagerly. The vision of Miss Farquharson, and her conviction of her cousin's innocence, had impressed me in her favour.

The professor scowled at me. 'How often am I to tell you that facts are all that matter?' he replied. 'Our journey tomorrow will be for the purpose of ascertaining facts. Until we know these, it would be waste of time to indulge in conjecture.'

He did not mention the subject again until the next morning, when we were seated in the train to Purfleet. He had chosen an empty first-class carriage, and himself took the right-hand corner facing the engine. He said nothing until the train was travelling at a good speed, and then he addressed me suddenly.

'You are a good shot with a rifle, are you not?' he inquired.

'I used to be pretty fair,' I replied in astonishment. 'But I don't think I've had a rifle in my hand since the war.'

'Well, take my stick, and hold it as you would a rifle. Now go to the far end of the carriage and lean against the door. That's right. Point your stick at my right eye, as though you were going to shoot at it. Stand like that a minute. Thank you, that will do.'

He turned away from me, took a pair of field-glasses from a case he was carrying, and began to survey the country through the window on his side. This he continued to do until the train drew up at Purfleet and we dismounted on to the platform.

'Ah, a lovely day!' he exclaimed. 'Not too warm for a little walking. We will make our first call at Purfleet ranges. This was where young Halliday came to do his shooting, you remember.'

We made our way to the ranges, and were lucky enough to find the warden at home. Dr Priestley had, when he chose, a most ingratiating way with him, and he and the warden were very shortly engaged in an animated conversation.

'By the way,' inquired the professor earnestly, 'was there any firing going on here between half-past two and three on Saturday last?'

The range-warden scratched his head with a thoughtful expression on his face. 'Let me see, now, last Saturday afternoon? We had a squad of Territorials here on Saturday afternoon, but they didn't arrive till after three. Lord, they was queer hands with a rifle, some of them. Much as they could do to hit the target at all at three hundred. They won't never make marksmen, however hard they try.'

'Isn't it rather dangerous to allow such wild shots to fire at all?' suggested the professor.

'God bless your heart, sir, it's safe enough,' replied the range-warden. 'There's never been an accident the whole time I've been here. They can't very well miss the butts, and even if they did, there's nobody allowed on the marshes when firing's going on.'

'That is comforting, certainly,' said the professor. 'Apart from this squad, you had nobody else?'

The range-warden shook his head. 'No, sir, they was the only people on the range that day.'

'I suppose it is part of your duty to issue ammunition?' inquired the professor.

'As a rule, sir. But, as it happens, this particular squad always brings their own with them.'

The professor continued his conversation for a little longer, then prepared to depart.

'I'm sure I'm very much obliged to you,' he said as he shook hands. 'By the way, I believe there are other ranges about here somewhere?'

'That's right, sir,' replied the range-warden. 'Over yonder, beyond the butts. Rainham ranges, they're called.'

'Is there any objection to my walking across the marshes to them?'

'Not a bit, sir. There's no firing today. Just keep straight on past the butts, and you'll come to them.'

The professor and I started on our tramp, the professor pausing every hundred yards or so to look about him through his field-glasses and to verify his position on the map. We reached the Rainham ranges at last, discovered the warden, who fell under the influence of the professor's charm as readily as his colleague at Purfleet had done, and opened the conversation with him in much the same style.

'On Saturday afternoon last, between half-past two and three?' replied the warden to the professor's inquiry. 'Well, sir, not what you might call any shooting. There was a party from Woolwich, with a new sort of light machine-gun, something like a Lewis. But they wasn't shooting, only testing.'

'What is the difference?' asked the professor.

'Well, sir, by testing I mean they had the thing held in a clamp, so that it couldn't move. The idea is to keep it pointing in exactly the same direction, instead of wobbling about as it might if a man was holding it. They use a special target, and measure up the distance between the various bullet-holes on it when they've finished.'

'I see,' replied the professor. 'I wonder if you would mind showing me where they were firing from?'

'Certainly, sir, it's close handy.' The range-warden led us to a firing-point near by, and pointed out the spot on which the stand had been erected.

'That's the place, sir. They were firing at number 10 target over yonder. A thousand yards it is, and wonderful accurate the new gun seemed. Shot the target to pieces they did.'

The professor made no reply, but took out his map and drew a line upon it from the firing-point to the butts. The line, when extended, led over a tract of desolate marshes until it met the river.

'There is very little danger on these ranges, it appears,' remarked the professor, with a note of annoyance in his voice. 'If a shot missed the butts altogether, it could only fall into the river, far away from any frequented spot.'

'That's what they were laid out for,' replied the range-warden. 'You see, on the other side there's a house or two, to say nothing of the road and the railway. It wouldn't do to have any stray rounds falling among them.'

'It certainly would not,' replied the professor absently. 'I see by the map that Rainham station is not far beyond the end of the ranges. Is there any objection to my walking to it past the butts?'

'None at all, sir, it's the best way to get there when there's no firing on. Thank you, sir, it's been no trouble at all.'

We started to walk down the ranges, a puzzled frown on the professor's face. Every few yards he stopped and examined the country through his glasses, or pulled out the map and stared at it with an absorbed expression. We had reached the butts before he said a word, and then it was not until we had climbed to the top of them that he spoke.

'Very puzzling, very!' he muttered. 'There must, of course, be some explanation. A mathematical deduction from facts can never be false. But I wish I could discover the explanation.'

He was looking through his field-glasses as he spoke, and suddenly his attention became riveted upon an object in front of him. Without waiting for me he hurried down the steep sides of the butts, and almost ran towards a flagstaff standing a couple of hundred yards on the far side of them. When he arrived at the base of it, he drew a couple of lines on the map, walked half round the flagstaff and gazed intently through his glasses. By the time I had caught up with him he had put the glasses back in their case, and was smiling benevolently.

'We can return to town by the next train, my boy,' he said cheerfully. 'I have ascertained everything I wished to know.'

He refused to say a word until our train was running into Fenchurch Street station. Then suddenly he turned to me.

'I am going to the War Office,' he said curtly. 'Will you go to Scotland Yard, see Inspector Hanslet, and ask him to come to Westbourne Terrace as soon as he can?'

I found Hanslet, after some little trouble, and gave him the professor's message.

'Something to do with the Farquharson business, I suppose?' he replied. ' Well, I'll come if the professor wants to see me. But I've got it all fixed up without his help.'

He turned up, true to his promise, and the professor greeted him with a pleasant smile.

'Good evening, inspector, I'm glad you were able to come. Will you be particularly busy tomorrow morning?'

'I don't think so, professor,' replied Hanslet in a puzzled voice. 'Do you want me to do anything?'

'Well, if you can spare the time, I should like to introduce you to the murderer of Mr Farquharson,' said the professor casually.

Hanslet lay back in his chair and laughed. 'Thanks very much, professor, but I've met him already,' he replied. 'It would be a waste of your time, I'm afraid.'

'Never mind,' said the professor, with a tolerant smile. ' I assure you that it will be worth your while to spend the morning with me. Will you meet me by the bookstall at Charing Cross at half-past ten?'

Hanslet reflected for a moment. The professor had never yet led him on a wild-goose chase, and it might be worth while to humour him.

'All right,' he replied reluctantly. 'I'll come. But I warn you it's no good.'

The professor smiled, but said nothing. Hanslet took his leave of us, and the professor appeared to put all thought of the Farquharson case out of his head.

We met again at Charing Cross the next day. The professor had taken tickets to Woolwich, and we got out of the train there and walked to the gates of the arsenal. The professor took an official letter out of his pocket, which he gave to the porter. In a few minutes we were led to an office, where a young officer rose to greet us.

'Good morning, Doctor Priestley,' he said. 'Colonel Conyngham rang me up to say that you were coming. You want to see the stand we use for testing the new automatic rifle? It happens to be in the yard below, being repaired.'

'Being repaired?' repeated the professor quickly. 'May I ask what is the matter with it?'

'Oh, nothing serious. We used it at Rainham the other day, and the clamp broke just as we were finishing a series. We had fired ninety-nine rounds out of a hundred, when the muzzle of the gun slipped up. I don't know what happened to the round. I suppose it went into the river somewhere. Beastly nuisance, we shall have to go down and start all over again.'

'Ah!' exclaimed the professor, in a satisfied tone. 'That explains it. But I wouldn't use number 10 target again, if I were you. Can we see this stand?'

'Certainly,' replied the officer. 'Come along.'

He led us into the yard, where a sort of tripod with a clamp at the head of it was standing. The professor looked at it earnestly for some moments, then turned to Hanslet.

'There you see the murderer of Mr Farquharson,' he said quietly.

Of course Hanslet, the officer, and myself bombarded him with questions, which he refused to answer until we had returned to London and were seated in his study. Then, fixing his eyes upon the ceiling and putting the tips of his fingers together, he began.

'It was, to any intelligent man, perfectly obvious that there are half a dozen reasons why young Halliday could not have shot his uncle. In the first place, he must have fired at very close range, from one side or other of the carriage, and a rifle bullet fired at such a range, although it very often makes a very extensive wound of entry, does not stay in a man's brain. It travels right through his head, with very slightly diminished velocity. Next, if Halliday fired at his uncle at all, it must have been from the left-hand side of the carriage. Had he fired from the right-hand side, the muzzle of the weapon would have been almost touching his victim, and there would have been signs of burning or blackening round the wound. Do you admit this, inspector?'

'Of course,' replied Hanslet. 'My theory always has been that he fired from the left-hand side.'

'Very well,' said the professor quickly. 'Now Halliday is notoriously a very bad shot, hence his journey to Purfleet. Harold, on the contrary, is a good shot. Yet, during our expedition of yesterday, I asked him to aim at my right eye with a stick while the train was in motion. I found that never for an instant could he point the stick at it. I find it impossible to believe that a bad shot, firing from the footboard and therefore compelled to use one hand at least to retain his hold, could shoot a man on the far side of the carriage exactly on the temple.'

The professor paused, and Hanslet looked at him doubtfully.

'It all sounds very plausible, professor, but until you can produce a better explanation I shall continue to believe that my own is the correct one.'

'Exactly. It was to verify a theory which I had formed that I carried out my investigations. It was perfectly obvious to me, from your description of the wound, that it had been inflicted by a bullet very near the end of its flight, and therefore possessing only enough velocity to penetrate the skull without passing through it. This meant that it had been fired from a considerable distance away. Upon consulting the map, I discovered that there were two rifle ranges near the railway between London and Tilbury. I could not help feeling that the source of the bullet was probably one of these ranges. It was, at all events, a possibility worth investigating.

'But at the outset I was faced with what seemed an insuperable objection. I deduced from the map, a deduction subsequently verified by examination of the ground, that a round fired at any of the targets on either range would take a direction away from the railway. I also discovered that the only rounds fired while the train in which Mr Farquharson's body was found was passing the ranges were by an experimental party from the arsenal. This party employed a special device which eliminated any inaccuracy due to the human element. At this point it occurred to me that my theory was incapable of proof, although I still adhered to my view that it was correct.'

The professor paused and Hanslet ventured to remark:

'I still do not see how you can prove that the breakage of the clamp could have been responsible,' he said. 'The direction of the bullet remained the same, and only its elevation was affected. By your own showing, the last shot fired from the machine must have landed in the marshes or the river.'

'I knew very well that notwithstanding the apparent impossibility, this must have been the bullet which killed Mr Farquharson,' replied the professor equably. 'I climbed the butts behind the target at which the arsenal party had been firing, and while there I made an interesting discovery which solved the difficulty at once. Directly in line with number 10 target and some distance behind it was a flagstaff. Further, upon examination of this flagstaff I discovered that it was made of steel.

'Now the map had told me that there was only a short stretch of line upon which a train could be struck by a bullet deflected by this flagstaff. If this had indeed been the case, I knew exactly where to look for traces, and at my first inspection I found them. High up on the staff is a scar where the paint has recently been removed. To my mind the cause of Mr Farquharson's death is adequately explained.'

Hanslet whistled softly. ' By Jove, there's something in it!' he exclaimed. 'Your theory, I take it, is that Farquharson was struck by a bullet deflected by the flagstaff?'

'Of course,' replied the professor. 'He was sitting on the right-hand side of the carriage, facing the engine. He was struck on the right side of the head, which supports the theory of a bullet coming through the open window. A bullet deflected in this way usually turns over and over for the rest of its flight, which accounts for the size of the wound. Have you any objection to offer?'

'Not at the moment,' said Hanslet cautiously. 'I shall have to verify all these facts, of course. For one thing, I must take the bullet to the arsenal and see if it is one of the same type as the experimental party were using.'

'Verify everything you can, certainly,' replied the professor. 'But remember that facts, not conjecture, are what should guide you.'

Hanslet nodded. 'I'll remember, professor,' he said. And with that he left us.

Two days later Mary announced Miss Farquharson and Mr Halliday. They entered the room, and Halliday walked straight up to the professor and grasped his hand.

'You have rendered me the greatest service one man can render to another, sir!' he exclaimed. ' Inspector Hanslet tells me that all suspicion that I murdered my uncle has been cleared away, and that this is due entirely to your efforts.'

Before the professor could reply, Miss Farquharson ran up to him and kissed him impulsively. 'Doctor Priestley, you're a darling!' she exclaimed.

The professor beamed at her through his spectacles. 'Really, my dear, you make me feel quite sorry that you are going to marry this young man,' he said.